LOTS OF SILLY JOKES FOR KIDS AGES 5-12

800 Funny Jokes About Cats, Dogs, Dinosaurs, Monsters, Music, Knock-knock, And More For Toddlers To Laugh And Have Fun With Their Parents.

Mahdi Amini

Introduction

Welcome, dear readers! If you're seeking a thrilling escape into the world of stories for kids and adults or if you're in the market for beautifully designed notebooks, I invite you to visit my author page. It's your gateway to a realm of chilling narratives and exquisite stationery.
Thank you "Mahdi Amini"

Please rate my book if you like it

Knock Knock Jokes

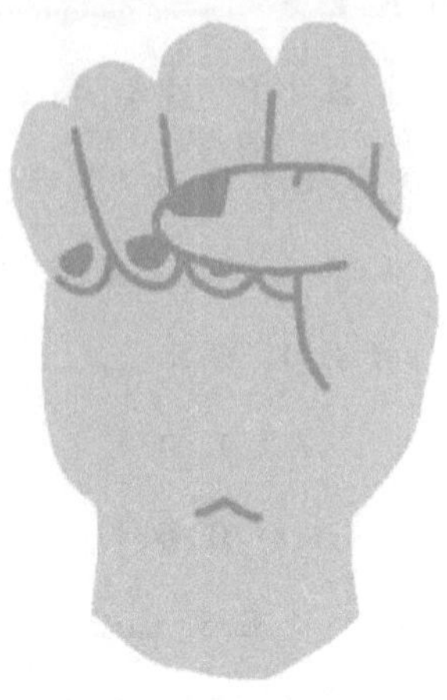

1. Knock, knock. Who's there? Meow. Meow who? Meow or never, I'm here to tell you a joke!

2. Knock, knock. Who's there? Kitten. Kitten who? Kitten your lap, ready for cuddles!

3. Knock, knock. Who's there? Paws. Paws who?

Paws and reflect on how purr-fect cats are!

4. Knock, knock. Who's there? Feline. Feline who? Feline fine and ready to purr-suade you with a joke!

5. Knock, knock. Who's there? Whiskers. Whiskers who? Whiskers the nearest cat, I've got more jokes to share!

6. Knock, knock. Who's there? Purr. Purr who? Purr-haps you're ready for another cat-tastic joke!

7. Knock, knock. Who's there? Tabby. Tabby who? Tabby honest, these

cat jokes are the best!

8. Knock, knock. Who's there? Kitty. Kitty who? Kitty bit of milk would make this joke even better!

9. Knock, knock. Who's there? Mew. Mew who? Mew-tiful day for some cat humor, isn't it?

10. Knock, knock. Who's there? Purrfect. Purrfect who? Purrfect time for a cat joke, don't you think?

11. Knock, knock. Who's there? Tail. Tail who? Tail me, are you ready for more cat jokes?

12. Knock, knock.

Who's there? Litter. Litter
who? Litter by little, we'll
tell more cat jokes!

13.   Knock, knock.
Who's there? Pounce.
Pounce who? Pounce on
the opportunity to hear
another cat joke!

14.   Knock, knock.
Who's there? Claws.
Claws who? Claws your
way into laughter with
this cat joke!

15.   Knock, knock.
Who's there? Kitty litter.
Kitty litter who? Kitty
litter sister, and she wants
to hear a joke too!

16.   Knock, knock.
Who's there? Meow-tain.

Meow-tain who? Meow-tain-ly, I'll tell you a cat joke!

17.   Knock, knock. Who's there? Purr-sistence. Purr-sistence who? Purr-sistence pays off, especially when it comes to jokes!

18.   Knock, knock. Who's there? Paw-ty. Paw-ty who? Paw-ty time with more cat jokes!

19.   Knock, knock. Who's there? Pawsitive. Pawsitive who? Pawsitive you'll love this next cat joke!

20.   Knock, knock. Who's there? Catnip.

Catnip who? Catnip a
cozy spot, and I'll tell you
one last cat joke!

21.   Knock, knock.
Who's there? Woof.
Woof who? Woof you
like to hear a funny dog
joke?

22.   Knock, knock.
Who's there? Bark. Bark
who? Bark up, it's time
for a doggone good joke!

23.   Knock, knock.
Who's there? Paws. Paws
who? Paws for effect,
I've got a great dog joke
for you!

24.   Knock, knock.
Who's there? Fido. Fido
who? Fido the door, now

let me in to tell you a
joke!

25.   Knock, knock.
Who's there? Rover.
Rover who? Rover here
to make you laugh with a
doggy joke!

26.   Knock, knock.
Who's there? Howl. Howl
who? Howl you know if
you don't hear the joke?

27.   Knock, knock.
Who's there? Biscuit.
Biscuit who? Biscuit the
door and fetch another
joke!

28.   Knock, knock.
Who's there? Collie.
Collie who? Collie-
lecting jokes, and here's a

good one!

29.   Knock, knock.
Who's there? Hound.
Hound who? Hound me
for more jokes, I've got
plenty!

30.   Knock, knock.
Who's there? Tail. Tail
who? Tail me a joke, and
I'll wag my tail!

31.   Knock, knock.
Who's there? Poodle.
Poodle who? Poodle-
icious joke coming right
up!

32.   Knock, knock.
Who's there? Barking.
Barking who? Barking up
the right door for another
joke!

33.   Knock, knock. Who's there? Sniff. Sniff who? Sniff around, there's more jokes to find!

34.   Knock, knock. Who's there? Lab. Lab who? Lab-radorable joke just for you!

35.   Knock, knock. Who's there? Terrier. Terrier who? Terrier-fic joke time!

36.   Knock, knock. Who's there? Beagle. Beagle who? Beagle-ieve me, this joke is funny!

37.   Knock, knock. Who's there? Dachshund. Dachshund who?

Dachshund the door and
let me tell you a joke!

38. Knock, knock.
Who's there? Husky.
Husky who? Husky up,
and I'll tell you a great
joke!

39. Knock, knock.
Who's there? Golden.
Golden who? Golden
opportunity for laughter
with this joke!

40. Knock, knock.
Who's there? Shih Tzu.
Shih Tzu who? Shih Tzu
good to be true, but here's
a joke for you!

41. Knock, knock.
Who's there?
Tyrannosaurus.

Tyrannosaurus who?
Tyrannosaurus-ically
funny dinosaur joke for
you!

42.   Knock, knock.
Who's there?
Stegosaurus. Stegosaurus
who? Stegosaurus you
ready for a dino-mite
joke?

43.   Knock, knock.
Who's there? Triceratops.
Triceratops who?
Triceratops and I'll tell
you a roaring good joke!

44.   Knock, knock.
Who's there? Pterodactyl.
Pterodactyl who?
Pterodactyl-y the coolest
dinosaur joke ever!

45.   Knock, knock.
Who's there? Raptor.
Raptor who? Raptor
presents and I'll tell you a
joke!

46.   Knock, knock.
Who's there?
Brachiosaurus.
Brachiosaurus who?
Brachiosaurus some
funny jokes for you!

47.   Knock, knock.
Who's there?
Velociraptor.
Velociraptor who?
Velociraptor and listen,
I've got a great joke!

48.   Knock, knock.
Who's there?
Archaeopteryx.
Archaeopteryx who?

Archaeopteryx-tremely
funny joke coming up!

49.   Knock, knock.
Who's there?
Spinosaurus. Spinosaurus
who? Spinosaurus time
for a hilarious joke!

50.   Knock, knock.
Who's there? Diplodocus.
Diplodocus who?
Diplodocus joke will
make you laugh!

51.   Knock, knock.
Who's there?
Ankylosaurus.
Ankylosaurus who?
Ankylosaurus and I'll
share a funny joke!

52.   Knock, knock.
Who's there? Allosaurus.

Allosaurus who?
Allosaurus jokes are the
best, don't you think?

53.   Knock, knock.
Who's there?
Brontosaurus.
Brontosaurus who?
Brontosaurus-ly funny
joke on its way!

54.   Knock, knock.
Who's there?
Dilophosaurus.
Dilophosaurus who?
Dilophosaurus-y good
joke for you!

55.   Knock, knock.
Who's there?
Carnotaurus. Carnotaurus
who? Carnotaurus is the
perfect time for a joke!

56.   Knock, knock.
Who's there? Iguanodon.
Iguanodon who?
Iguanodon-za joke for
you to enjoy!

57.   Knock, knock.
Who's there?
Velociraptor.
Velociraptor who?
Velociraptor-ove another
dinosaur joke!

58.   Knock, knock.
Who's there?
Micropachycephalosauru
s.
Micropachycephalosauru
s who?
Micropachycephalosauru
s-tastic joke for you!

59.   Knock, knock.
Who's there?

Brachiosaurus.
Brachiosaurus who?
Brachiosaurus and tell
you a funny joke!

60.	Knock, knock.
Who's there? T-Rex. T-
Rex who? T-Rex to laugh
with this hilarious
dinosaur joke!

61.	Knock, knock.
Who's there?
Tyrannosaurus.
Tyrannosaurus who?
Tyrannosaurus-ically
funny dinosaur joke for
you!

62.	Knock, knock.
Who's there?
Stegosaurus. Stegosaurus
who? Stegosaurus you
ready for a dino-mite

joke?

63.	Knock, knock.
Who's there? Triceratops.
Triceratops who?
Triceratops and I'll tell
you a roaring good joke!

64.	Knock, knock.
Who's there? Pterodactyl.
Pterodactyl who?
Pterodactyl-y the coolest
dinosaur joke ever!

65.	Knock, knock.
Who's there? Raptor.
Raptor who? Raptor
presents and I'll tell you a
joke!

66.	Knock, knock.
Who's there?
Brachiosaurus.
Brachiosaurus who?

Brachiosaurus some
funny jokes for you!

67.   Knock, knock.
Who's there?
Velociraptor.
Velociraptor who?
Velociraptor and listen,
I've got a great joke!

68.   Knock, knock.
Who's there?
Archaeopteryx.
Archaeopteryx who?
Archaeopteryx-tremely
funny joke coming up!

69.   Knock, knock.
Who's there?
Spinosaurus. Spinosaurus
who? Spinosaurus time
for a hilarious joke!

70.   Knock, knock.

Who's there? Diplodocus.
Diplodocus who?
Diplodocus joke will
make you laugh!

71.   Knock, knock.
Who's there?
Ankylosaurus.
Ankylosaurus who?
Ankylosaurus and I'll
share a funny joke!

72.   Knock, knock.
Who's there? Allosaurus.
Allosaurus who?
Allosaurus jokes are the
best, don't you think?

73.   Knock, knock.
Who's there?
Brontosaurus.
Brontosaurus who?
Brontosaurus-ly funny
joke on its way!

74.	Knock, knock.
Who's there?
Dilophosaurus.
Dilophosaurus who?
Dilophosaurus-y good
joke for you!

75.	Knock, knock.
Who's there?
Carnotaurus. Carnotaurus
who? Carnotaurus is the
perfect time for a joke!

76.	Knock, knock.
Who's there? Iguanodon.
Iguanodon who?
Iguanodon-za joke for
you to enjoy!

77.	Knock, knock.
Who's there?
Velociraptor.
Velociraptor who?
Velociraptor-ove another

dinosaur joke!

78.   Knock, knock.
Who's there?
Micropachycephalosauru
s.
Micropachycephalosauru
s who?
Micropachycephalosauru
s-tastic joke for you!

79.   Knock, knock.
Who's there?
Brachiosaurus.
Brachiosaurus who?
Brachiosaurus and tell
you a funny joke!

80.   Knock, knock.
Who's there? T-Rex. T-
Rex who? T-Rex to laugh
with this hilarious
dinosaur joke!

81.   Knock, knock.
Who's there? Lettuce.
Lettuce who? Lettuce in;
it's too cold to learn
outside!

82.   Knock, knock.
Who's there? Alpaca.
Alpaca who? Alpaca the
books, it's time for
school!

83.   Knock, knock.
Who's there? Dewey.
Dewey who? Dewey
have to go to school
today?

84.   Knock, knock.
Who's there? Spell. Spell
who? W-H-O.

85.   Knock, knock.
Who's there? Principal.
Principal who? Principal
teacher wants to see you
in the office!

86.   Knock, knock.
Who's there? Abby. Abby
who? Abby to school, I'm
running late!
87.   Knock, knock.
Who's there? Hannah.
Hannah who? Hannah
parrot in our class!
88.   Knock, knock.
Who's there? Dinah.
Dinah who? Dinah think
school is fun?
89.   Knock, knock.
Who's there? Ima. Ima
who? Ima gonna do my
homework now!
90.   Knock, knock.
Who's there? Olive. Olive
who? Olive your
textbooks are in your
backpack!
91.   Knock, knock.
Who's there? Howard.

Howard who? Howard
you like to go to school
today?

92.   Knock, knock.
Who's there? Dewey.
Dewey who? Dewey
have to do homework
again?

93.   Knock, knock.
Who's there? Justin.
Justin who? Just in time
for the school bus!

94.   Knock, knock.
Who's there? Anna. Anna
who? Anna teacher will
be mad if we're late!

95.   Knock, knock.
Who's there? Andy. Andy
who? Andy last bell
rings, it's time for recess!

96.   Knock, knock.
Who's there? Donut.

Donut who? Donut forget your lunchbox!

97.   Knock, knock. Who's there? School. School who? School's in session, time to learn!

98.   Knock, knock. Who's there? B-2. B-2 who? B-2 school, don't be late!

99.   Knock, knock. Who's there? Cow says. Cow says who? No, silly, cow says moo!

100.   Knock, knock. Who's there? Owl. Owl who? Owl be so happy when the school day is over!

101.   Knock, knock. Who's there? Orange. Orange who? Orange you

glad we have more jokes
to tell?

102.	Knock, knock.
Who's there? Blue. Blue
who? Blue your nose and
let's keep the laughs
coming!

103.	Knock, knock.
Who's there? Pink. Pink
who? Pink your funniest
face; it's joke time!

104.	Knock, knock.
Who's there? Green.
Green who? Green with
envy because my jokes
are so funny!

105.	Knock, knock.
Who's there? Maroon.
Maroon who? Marooned
in laughter with these
hilarious jokes!

106.	Knock, knock.
Who's there? Silver.

Silver who? Silver lining:
these jokes are pure gold!

107.   Knock, knock.
Who's there? Red. Red
who? Red-y or not, here
comes a funny joke!

108.   Knock, knock.
Who's there? Lavender.
Lavender who?
Lavender-tly, these jokes
are making you laugh!

109.   Knock, knock.
Who's there? Yellow.
Yellow who? Yellow-
ways enjoy a good joke!

110.   Knock, knock.
Who's there? Turquoise.
Turquoise who?
Turquoise-y and laughter
is the best medicine!

111.   Knock, knock.
Who's there? Teal. Teal

who? Teal the spotlight;
it's joke time!

112.   Knock, knock.
Who's there? Gold. Gold
who? Gold-old your
laughter; here comes a
great joke!

113.   Knock, knock.
Who's there? Indigo.
Indigo who? Indigo every
time I tell a joke, it's a
hit!

114.   Knock, knock.
Who's there? Beige.
Beige who? Beige ready
for some side-splitting
jokes!

115.   Knock, knock.
Who's there? Plum. Plum
who? Plum crazy for
these funny jokes!

116.   Knock, knock.
Who's there? Charcoal.

Charcoal who? Charcoal-ways great to laugh with you!

117.   Knock, knock. Who's there? Mauve. Mauve who? Mauve-lous jokes coming your way!

118.   Knock, knock. Who's there? Paprika. Paprika who? Paprika-lly, this joke is a spice of humor!

119.   Knock, knock. Who's there? Coral. Coral who? Coral-ious jokes are the best kind!

120.   Knock, knock. Who's there? Lemon. Lemon who? Lemon-squeeze in more laughs with this joke!

121.   Knock, knock. Who's there? Frank.

Frank who?
Frankenstein, here to tell
you a monstrously funny
joke!

122.   Knock, knock.
Who's there? Boo. Boo
who? Don't cry; it's just a
friendly monster joke!

123.   Knock, knock.
Who's there? Igor. Igor
who? Igor to tell you a
hilarious monster joke!

124.   Knock, knock.
Who's there? Mummy.
Mummy who? Mummy
pleased to make you
laugh with this joke!

125.   Knock, knock.
Who's there? Dracula.
Dracula who? Dracula-
some laughs from this
spooky vampire!

126.   Knock, knock.
Who's there? Ghoul.
Ghoul who? Ghoul-tide
cheer with a funny joke
for you!

127.   Knock, knock.
Who's there? Cyclops.
Cyclops who? Cyclops
on a good joke when I
see one!

128.   Knock, knock.
Who's there? Zombie.
Zombie who? Zombie
glad you're here for a
joke!

129.   Knock, knock.
Who's there? Ogre. Ogre
who? Ogrejoy sharing
funny jokes with you!

130.   Knock, knock.
Who's there? Yeti. Yeti
who? Yeti another
hilarious joke for you!

131.   Knock, knock.
Who's there? Werewolf.
Werewolf who?
Werewolf down with
laughter from this joke!

132.   Knock, knock.
Who's there? Wraith.
Wraith who? Wraith for
it... here comes a funny
joke!

133.   Knock, knock.
Who's there? Phantom.
Phantom who? Phantom-
tastic joke coming up!

134.   Knock, knock.
Who's there? Banshee.
Banshee who? Banshee-
ning your day with a
funny joke!

135.   Knock, knock.
Who's there? Ghost.
Ghost who? Ghost to

show you this joke is a
scream!

136.   Knock, knock.
Who's there? Poltergeist.
Poltergeist who?
Poltergeist your fears
with humor!

137.   Knock, knock.
Who's there? Manticore.
Manticore who?
Manticore funny jokes
for you to enjoy!

138.   Knock, knock.
Who's there? Harpy.
Harpy who? Harpy to tell
you a great monster joke!

139.   Knock, knock.
Who's there? Troll. Troll
who? Troll-ific jokes
await, so get ready to
laugh!

140.   Knock, knock.
Who's there? Wight.

Wight who? Wight here with a funny joke for you!

141.   Knock, knock. Who's there? Tennis. Tennis who? Tennis anyone? I'm ready to tell a funny sports joke!

142.   Knock, knock. Who's there? Soccer. Soccer who? Soccer be another great joke on its way!

143.   Knock, knock. Who's there? Golf. Golf who? Golfing to tell you a hole-in-one joke!

144.   Knock, knock. Who's there? Baseball. Baseball who? Baseball you a question: Are you ready to laugh?

145.   Knock, knock.
Who's there? Swimming.
Swimming who?
Swimming great jokes
are just a splash away!

146.   Knock, knock.
Who's there? Volleyball.
Volleyball who?
Volleyball to make you
smile with a funny joke!

147.   Knock, knock.
Who's there? Football.
Football who? Football
me, I've got a touchdown
of a joke!

148.   Knock, knock.
Who's there? Hockey.
Hockey who? Hockey
time for another sports
joke!

149.   Knock, knock.
Who's there? Basketball.
Basketball who?

Basketball you like to
hear a slam-dunk joke?

150.   Knock, knock.
Who's there? Running.
Running who? Running
to tell you a fast and
funny joke!

151.   Knock, knock.
Who's there? Bowling.
Bowling who? Bowling
you over with a hilarious
joke!

152.   Knock, knock.
Who's there? Surfing.
Surfing who? Surfing up
some great laughs with
this joke!

153.   Knock, knock.
Who's there? Skiing.
Skiing who? Skiing great
jokes down the slopes of
humor!

154.   Knock, knock.
Who's there? Racing.
Racing who? Racing to
tell you a speedy joke!

155.   Knock, knock.
Who's there?
Gymnastics. Gymnastics
who? Gymnastics a
funny joke for you to
enjoy!

156.   Knock, knock.
Who's there? Cricket.
Cricket who? Cricket's
chirping with laughter
from this joke!

157.   Knock, knock.
Who's there? Badminton.
Badminton who?
Badminton-tastic joke on
its way!

158.   Knock, knock.
Who's there? Javelin.

Javelin who? Javelin you
a funny sports joke!
159.   Knock, knock.
Who's there? Archery.
Archery who? Archery-
typal joke for some
bullseye laughs!
160.   Knock, knock.
Who's there? Racing.
Racing who? Racing the
clock to share this joke
with you!

Underwater Jokes

161. Why did the fish blush? Because it saw the ocean's bottom!

162. What do you call a fish that wears a crown? King Neptune-tune!

163. How do you organize a party for a school of fish? You let

them have a "reef"-
reshment table!

164.   What do you call a
crab that never shares?
Shellfish!

165.   Why don't seagulls
fly over the bay? Because
then they'd be called
"bagels"!

166.   What did one
underwater creature say
to the other? "You're a
great "fin"d!"

167.   Why don't oysters
donate to charity?
Because they are
shellfish!

168.   What do you call a
shark that's good at math?
An "alge-bro!"

169.   How do you
communicate with a fish?
You drop it a line!

170.   What did the ocean say to the beach? Nothing, it just waved!

171.   Why did the starfish put sunscreen on the computer? Because it wanted to avoid getting a "screen burn"!

172.   What do you call a fish that performs magic tricks? A "pufferfish"ionist!

173.   What's a dolphin's favorite game? Squid and seek!

174.   How do you make an octopus laugh? With ten-tickles!

175.   What do you call a fish that practices medicine? A sturgeon!

176.   Why did the seahorse sit at the bottom

of the ocean? Because it didn't want to rise to the surface!

177.   What's a shark's favorite candy? Swedish Fish!

178.   How do fish stay healthy? They do "waterobics"!

179.   What's a mermaid's favorite instrument? The harp-sea-chord!

180.   Why don't fish do well in school? Because they're always swimming below "sea" level!

Cat Jokes

181. Why was the cat sitting next to the computer? Because it wanted to keep an eye on the mouse!

182. What do you get if you cross a cat with a fish? A purrmaid!

183. How does a cat end a fight? It says, "That's claw-ver enough for me!"

184.   What do you call a
cat that can sing? A furr-
midable vocalist!

185.   Why did the cat
bring a ladder to the bar?
It heard the drinks were
on the house!

186.   What do you call a
cat magician? A purr-
former!

187.   How do cats end a
race? They use their
"purr-sistence"!

188.   What do you call a
cat that can play the
guitar? An acousticat!

189.   What do you call a
cat that's been caught by
the police? The purr-
petrator!

190.   Why did the cat put
the letter "M" into the
fridge? Because it wanted

to turn "ice cream" into "mice cream"!

191.   How does a cat get its own way? With friendly purrsuasion!

192.   What kind of cat loves water? An octo-puss!

193.   Why did the cat go to the barber? It needed a "purr"-fect haircut!

194.   How do you know if your cat is smart? It's always feline fine!

195.   What do you call a cat that can fly? A hot "air" balloon!

196.   What's a cat's favorite button on the remote control? Paws!

197.   What do you call a cat that can tell time? A meow-tician!

198.   How do cats write books? With their purr-sonalities!

199.   What do you call a cat that's a great detective? Sherlock Meow-lmes!

200.   What's a cat's favorite subject in school? Meow-sic!

Dog Jokes

201.   Why did the dog sit in the shade? Because he didn't want to be a hot dog!

202.   What do you call a dog magician? A labracadabrador!

203.   How do you make a dog stop barking in the front yard? Put him in the backyard!

204.   What's a dog's favorite instrument? The trombone!

205.   Why was the Dachshund always confident? He had a long "paws-itive" attitude!

206.   What kind of dog loves to take a bath? A shampoo-dle!

207.   How do you know if your dog is an archaeologist? He's always digging up the past!

208.   Why do dogs never use computers? Because they're afraid of the "mouse"!

209.   What did the dog say to the tree? "Bark!"

210.   What do you call a
dog who loves to bowl?
A strike retriever!

211.   Why don't dogs use
cell phones? Because
they can't find the "bark"
button!

212.   How do you catch a
squirrel? Climb a tree and
act like a nut!

213.   What's a dog's
favorite dessert?
Pupcakes!

214.   What did one dog
say to the other at the
movies? "I hope they
have 'bark-b-q' popcorn!"

215.   How does a dog stop
a video game? He presses
paws!

216.   What do you get
when you cross a dog and

a phone? A golden receiver!

217.   Why did the dog sit in the shade? Because he didn't want to be a "hot dog"!

218.   What's a dog's favorite kind of pizza? Pupperoni!

219.   How do you know if your dog is an opera singer? He hits all the high "barks"!

220.   What do you call a dog who's a famous rapper? Snoop Doggy Dog!

PlaceJokes

221. Why don't skeletons fight each other in the desert? Because they don't have the guts!

222. What's the happiest city in the world? Smiles-ington!

223. What do you call a fish who wears a crown? The king of the aquarium!

224. Where do snowmen go to dance? The snowball!

225. What's a pirate's favorite city? Arrrrrr-lanta!

226. Why did the math book look sad when it went on vacation?

Because it had too many problems!

227.   What did the big flower say to the little flower? "Hi, bud!"

228.   Where do pencils go for vacation? Pencil-vania!

229.   What's a cow's favorite place to go for fun? The moo-vies!

230.   Where do rabbits stay on vacation? In a harebnb!

231.   Why did the bicycle fall over in Amsterdam? Because it was two-tired!

232.   What's a ghost's favorite city? Boo-ston!

233.   Where do bees go on vacation? Stingapore!

234.   Why did the tomato turn red? Because it saw the salad dressing!

235.   Where do spiders go on their summer vacation? The web!

236.   What's a mummy's favorite vacation spot? Wrap-around-the-world tours!

237.   Why was the math book always ready for a trip? It had too many problems!

238.   What's a vampire's favorite place in New York? The Vampire State Building!

239.   Where do birds go on vacation? Finch-iti!

240.   What do you call a potato's favorite vacation spot? Idaho!

Movie Jokes

241.   Why don't skeletons fight each other in the desert? Because they don't have the guts!

242.   What's the happiest city in the world? Smiles-ington!

243.   What do you call a fish who wears a crown? The king of the aquarium!

244.   Where do snowmen go to dance? The snowball!

245.   What's a pirate's favorite city? Arrrrrr-lanta!

246.   Why did the math book look sad when it went on vacation? Because it had too many problems!

247.   What did the big flower say to the little flower? "Hi, bud!"

248.   Where do pencils go for vacation? Pencil-vania!

249.   What's a cow's favorite place to go for fun? The moo-vies!

250.   Where do rabbits stay on vacation? In a harebnb!

251.   Why did the bicycle fall over in Amsterdam? Because it was two-tired!

252.   What's a ghost's favorite city? Boo-ston!

253.   Where do bees go on vacation? Stingapore!

254.   Why did the tomato turn red? Because it saw the salad dressing!

255.   Where do spiders go on their summer vacation? The web!

256.   What's a mummy's favorite vacation spot? Wrap-around-the-world tours!

257.   Why was the math book always ready for a trip? It had too many problems!

258.   What's a vampire's favorite place in New York? The Vampire State Building!

259.   Where do birds go
on vacation? Finch-iti!

260.   What do you call a
potato's favorite vacation
spot? Idaho!

Dinosaur Jokes

261. What do you call a dinosaur with an extensive vocabulary? A thesaurus!

262. What do you call a dinosaur that's sleeping? A dino-snore!

263. How do you know there's a dinosaur in your fridge? Footprints in the butter!

264.   Why can't you hear a pterodactyl using the bathroom? Because the "P" is silent!

265.   What do you call a dinosaur with an extensive vocabulary? A thesaurus!

266.   What's a dinosaur's least favorite reindeer? Comet!

267.   Why did the dinosaur apply for a job? Because it was a little "dino-sore!"

268.   How do you make a dinosaur float? Add two scoops of ice cream and some root beer.

269.   What do you call a dinosaur with an excellent vocabulary and

grammar skills? A wordasaurus!

270.   Why did the dinosaur go to the doctor? Because it was dino-sick!

271.   What do you call a dinosaur with an amazing personality? A "dino-mite"!

272.   How do you ask a T-Rex to lunch? "Tea-Rex?"

273.   What do you call a dinosaur that's always late? A "dino-tardy"!

274.   What do you get when you cross a dinosaur with fireworks? Dino-mite!

275.   Why don't you ever hear a dinosaur tell a

secret? Because they're all dead!

276. What do you call a dinosaur that's a famous musician? A dino-saur!

277. How do you make a dinosaur stop charging? You take away its credit card!

278. What do you call a dinosaur with an extensive vinyl record collection? A "rock"osaurus!

279. Why did the dinosaur turn on the air conditioning? Because it was getting too hot to "dino-snore"!

280. What did the dinosaur use to fix its house? Dino-saw-ers!

School Jokes

281. Why did the math book look sad? Because it had too many problems!

282. What kind of snack do you eat in the library? Quiet chips!

283. Why was the computer cold? It left its Windows open!

284. How do you catch a squirrel at school? Climb a tree and act like a nut!

285.   Why did the
scarecrow become a
successful student?
Because he was
outstanding in his field!

286.   Why did the student
bring a ladder to school?
Because they wanted to
go to high school!

287.   Why don't scientists
trust atoms? Because
they make up everything!

288.   Why did the pencil
go to school? To get a
little sharper!

289.   What kind of school
do you learn to make ice
cream? Sundae school!

290.   What's a skeleton's
least favorite room in
school? The cafeteria,
because there's no body
to eat with!

291.   Why did the music teacher go to jail? Because she got caught with sharp objects!

292.   What do you call a bear that's a straight-A student? A bear-y smart!

293.   What did the math book say to the history book? "You're full of dates!"

294.   Why did the student take a ladder to school? Because they thought it was high school!

295.   What did the one wall say to the other wall in school? "I'll meet you at the corner!"

296.   Why did the broom get a gold star at school? Because it always swept the competition!

297.	Why did the kid
bring a ladder to school?
Because they thought it
was high school!

298.	What kind of tree
fits in your hand? A palm
tree, perfect for taking
notes in class!

299.	What's a vampire's
favorite subject in
school? Blood type!

300.	Why did the teacher
go to the beach? To test
the waters!

Holiday jokes

301. Why did the turkey go to the holiday party? To prove it wasn't chicken!

302. What do you call a snowman on rollerblades? Frostbite!

303. Why don't oysters share their pearls during

the holidays? Because they're a little shellfish!

304. How do snowmen get around during the holiday season? By riding "frosted" flakes!

305. What do you call a cat on the beach during the holidays? Sandy Claws!

306. Why did the gingerbread man go to therapy during the holidays? He felt a little crumby!

307. What's a reindeer's favorite type of music? "Wrap" music!

308. How does a snowman get around? By riding an "icicle"!

309.   Why did the Christmas tree go to the barber? It needed a trim!

310.   What do you call a snowman party? A snowball!

311.   What do you get if you cross a snowman and a dog during the holidays? Frostbite!

312.   Why did the ornament go to school? It wanted to get a little "tree-education"!

313.   What do you call a snowman with a six-pack? An abdominal snowman!

314.   What do you call a snowman with a carrot nose and a red scarf? Frosty the "Ro-man"!

315.   Why did the turkey sit on the tomahawk during Thanksgiving? To try to hatchet some holiday fun!

316.   How do you greet a snowman on the holiday? "Ice to meet you!"

317.   What do you call a snowman with a big ego? "Snow-It-All"!

318.   What's a snowman's favorite breakfast during the holidays? Ice Krispies!

319.   Why was the holiday tree so bad at sewing? It kept dropping its needles!

320.   What do you call a snowman in the summer? A puddle!

Car Jokes

321. Why did the car's engine go to school? To get a little "auto"-education!

322. What do you call a car that's feeling blue? An "emo-car."

323. What do you call a car that's been abandoned? A "car-gone."

324. Why did the car apply for a job? It wanted to quit being a "station-ary" vehicle!

325.   What kind of car does a Jedi drive? A "Toy-Yoda."

326.   Why was the car always smiling? Because it had great "brakes"!

327.   How do you make a car sound louder? Put your foot "down" on the gas pedal!

328.   What do you call a car that belongs to a sheep? A "Lamb"-orghini.

329.   Why did the car bring a blanket to the race? It wanted to stay "warm" during the laps!

330.   What kind of car is the most musical? A "Jazz" car!

331.   What do you get when you cross a car

with a kangaroo? A
jump-start!

332.   How does a car cool
down on a hot day? It
rolls down the
"windows."

333.   What did the traffic
light say to the car?
"Don't look now, but I'm
changing!"

334.   Why did the car visit
the doctor? It had a
"cough"-engine problem.

335.   How do you make a
tissue dance in a car? Put
a little boogie in it!

336.   What's a car's
favorite TV show?
"Wheel of Fortune."

337.   What's a race car's
favorite music? Anything
with "fast" beats!

338.   How does a car's
computer catch a virus? It
catches a "byte"!

339.   Why did the bicycle
bring a car to the race?
Because it wanted a
"two"-tire victory!

340.   What do you call a
car that's parked on the
street? A "parallel"
parked car!

UFO Jokes

341.   Why did the UFO bring a map to Earth? It didn't want to get lost in space traffic!

342.   What do you call an alien who loves to tell jokes? A "laughing saucer."

343.   How do you communicate with a friendly UFO? You "unidentified flying

offer" them some space snacks!

344.   Why did the UFO apply for a job? It wanted to earn some "flying saucers."

345.   What do you call a group of UFOs? A "flying saucer party"!

346.   How do you know if an alien visited your school? You spot unfamiliar "class-mates."

347.   What do UFOs use to play music? Flying saucer drums!

348.   Why did the UFO bring a pencil and paper? It wanted to "document" its visit!

349.   How do UFOs apologize? They say, "I'm so space-y!"

350.   What's an alien's favorite candy on Halloween? Mars bars!

351.   What did the UFO say to the airplane? "You're a down-to-earth vehicle."

352.   What do you call a UFO with a broken GPS? A "lost-astronaut"!

353.   How do you know when an alien is mad? It becomes "inter-galactically upset."

354.   Why do aliens like to read books upside down? Because it's an "unearthly" perspective!

355.   What's an alien's favorite game? Space invaders!

356.   Why did the UFO become a DJ? It wanted

to spin some "cosmic" tunes!

357.   How do aliens send secret messages? They use "Martian code"!

358.   What do you call a UFO that's a great dancer? An "astro-notable"!

359.   Why did the UFO visit the bakery? It wanted to try some "moon-pies"!

360.   How do you make a UFO laugh? Tell it a "comet-ic" joke!

Space jokes

361. Why did the sun go to school? To get a little brighter!

362. How do you throw a space party? You "planet" in advance!

363. What did the astronaut use to keep his pants up? An asteroid belt!

364. What kind of music do planets listen to? Neptunes!

365.   Why did the astronaut break up with his computer? It had too many space bars!

366.   What's a space pirate's favorite letter? "Arrrrrr!"

367.   What do you call a spaceship that's hard to find? A "disguisedcovery"!

368.   How do you organize a space picnic? You "comet" up with a plan!

369.   What do you call an alien chef? An "extraterrestri-cook"!

370.   How does the sun stay cool? It uses "solar" power!

371.   What do astronauts put in their coffee?

"Universe" sugar and "milky" way cream!

372.   Why did the astronaut break up with his girlfriend? He needed space!

373.   How does a spaceman get ready for a party? He "rockets" out with style!

374.   What do you call a monster from space? An "extraterrestri-grrr"!

375.   What do you call a planet that farts? Uranus!

376.   Why did the astronaut break the law? He needed to "asteroid" it out!

377.   How do you throw a successful meteor shower? You aim for the stars!

378.   What did one star
        say to the other? "You're
        a real star, you light up
        the galaxy!"
379.   Why don't planets
        ever get into trouble?
        Because they always
        follow their orbit!
380.   What do astronauts
        put in their sandwiches?
        "Launch" meat and
        "cosmo-cheese"!

Birthday Jokes

381. Why did the birthday cake go to the doctor? Because it was feeling crumby!

382. What do you give a lemon on its birthday? Lemon-aid!

383. Why did the boy bring a ladder to his

birthday party? Because
he wanted to go to new
heights!

384.   What did one candle
say to the other? "Don't
birthdays just burn you
up?"

385.   What do you get
when you cross a
birthday and a circus?
The greatest birthday
show on Earth!

386.   Why did the
computer go to the
birthday party? It wanted
to have byte-sized fun!

387.   What's a cat's
favorite dessert on its
birthday? Mice cream
and cake!

388.   Why did the teddy
bear say no to birthday

cake? Because it was stuffed!

389.	What's a vampire's favorite type of birthday cake? Devil's food cake!

390.	Why was the math book sad on its birthday? Because it had too many problems!

391.	What do you call a train full of bubblegum on its birthday? Chew-chew train!

392.	Why did the balloon bring a pin to the birthday party? It wanted to be a pop star!

393.	What's a tree's favorite part of a birthday party? The root beer!

394.	How do you know when you've had too much birthday cake?

When you can't see the
candles anymore!

395.   What did one wall
say to the other at the
birthday party? "I'll meet
you at the corner!"

396.   Why don't skeletons
go to birthday parties?
They have no body to go
with!

397.   What do you say to
your sister on her
birthday? "You're the
best, sis-treat ever!"

398.   Why did the bicycle
fall over at the birthday
party? Because it was
two-tired!

399.   What do you get
when you cross a
birthday with a pirate? A
birthday matey!

400.   Why did the tomato turn red at the birthday party? Because it saw the salad dressing!

Insect Jokes

401. What do you call an ant who likes to dance? A jitterbug!

402. Why did the firefly bring a flashlight to the insect party? It wanted to be a brighter bug!

403. What's a mosquito's favorite sport? Skin diving!

404. What do you call a bee that comes from

America? USB (United States Bee)!

405.   How do you send a letter to a grasshopper? Use "hopper" mail!

406.   Why did the spider go on the internet? It wanted to check its website!

407.   What do you call a fly without wings? A walk!

408.   Why don't bugs play hide and seek with beetles? Because they always find them in a "colony"!

409.   What do you call a ladybug who loves the beach? Sandy!

410.   What's a flea's favorite movie? Itching to Get Out!

411.   How do insects communicate? With their "ant"-tennas!

412.   What do you call a fly that likes to play basketball? A jump shot!

413.   Why did the caterpillar go to the dentist? It needed to get its "teeth" cleaned!

414.   What do you call a bee that can't make up its mind? Maybe!

415.   What's a butterfly's favorite subject in school? Mothematics!

416.   How do you organize a bug party? You send out "ant"-vitations!

417.   What's a mosquito's favorite song? "Bite Me Baby One More Time!"

418.   Why did the grasshopper start a band? Because it had the drumsticks!

419.   What do you get when you cross a spider and an owl? A web designer!

420.   How do you make an insect turn the other way? Just tell it to "bug off"!

Season Jokes

421. What did one autumn leaf say to another? "I'm falling for you!"

422. Why did the snowman bring a broom to the winter party? Because he wanted to sweep everyone off their feet!

423. What season is the best to go on a trampoline? Spring!

424. Why was the math book sad in the summer? Because it had too many problems to solve!

425. What season is it when you're on a trampoline? Spring-ting!

426.   What's a scarecrow's favorite season? Fall, because it's the time for "harvesting" compliments!

427.   Why did the scarecrow win an award in the spring? Because he was outstanding in his field!

428.   What did one snowman say to the other? "Do you smell carrots?"

429.   What's a tree's favorite season? Fall, because it gets to "leaf" things behind!

430.   Why do birds fly south for the winter? Because it's too far to walk!

431.   What's the favorite fruit of summer? Water-melon!

432.   Why did the sun go to school in the summer? To get a little brighter!

433.   What did the beach say as the tide came in? Long time no sea!

434.   What season is it when you are on a swing? Fall, because that's when the leaves "fall" down!

435.   Why do snowmen love to knit? Because they're so good at making "frosty" scarves!

436.   What season is it when you're too much of a fan? Fall, because you "fall" over with excitement!

437. Why did the bicycle
fall over in the winter?
Because it was two-tired!

438. What's a calendar's
favorite season? Spring,
because it has dates!

439. Why don't skeletons
go out in the winter?
Because they'd rather
stay chilled to the bone!

440. What did the winter
hat say to the scarf? "You
hang around; I'll cover
for you!"

Robot Jokes

441.   Why did the robot go on a diet? It had too many gigabytes!

442.   What do you call a robot that always tells the truth? Honest Iron!

443.   How do robots pay for things? With cache!

444.   Why did the robot bring a ladder to school? Because it wanted to go to high school!

445.   What do you call a robot that takes a nap? A "robo-snorer"!

446.   Why did the robot stand in front of the computer? It wanted to keep an eye on the mouse!

447.   How do you make a robot laugh? Tell it a byte-sized joke!

448.   What do you call a robot who loves to take photos? A "shutter bot"!

449.   What did the robot do when it had a cold? It took byte-sized tissues!

450.   Why did the robot go to the store? It wanted to upgrade its software wardrobe!

451.   What's a robot's favorite type of music? Heavy metal!

452.   How do you fix a broken robot? With a robot wrench!

453.   What do you call a robot with a sense of humor? A "joke bot"!

454.   Why don't robots play hide and seek? Because good luck hiding with all those shiny parts!

455.   What do robots eat for lunch? A byte of RAMen!

456.   How do you make a robot giggle? Tickle its funny bone!

457.   What do you call a robot that likes to tell stories? A "data-tale" bot!

458.   What's a robot's favorite game? Hide and circuit seek!

459.   What did the robot say to the computer? "I think I've lost my byte!"

460.   Why did the robot bring a can opener to school? Because it wanted to be "extra sharp"!

Music Jokes

461.   Why did the music teacher go to jail? Because she got caught with too many sharp objects!

462.   What do you get when you drop a piano down a mine shaft? A flat minor.

463.   What's a skeleton's least favorite room in the house? The living room.

464.   How do you fix a
broken tuba? With a tuba
glue.

465.   Why was the music
book always happy?
Because it had many
notes to play!

466.   What do you call a
bear that loves music? A
"bearitone."

467.   What's a cow's
favorite musical note?
Moo-sic!

468.   What did one wall
say to the other? "I'll
meet you at the corner!"

469.   What's a musician's
favorite fruit? A
"bananadrum."

470.   Why was the music
note a great friend?
Because it was always
there when you needed it!

471.   How do you make a tissue dance? Put a little boogie in it!

472.   What's a computer's favorite music genre? A "rom-com" (romantic comedy).

473.   Why don't skeletons play music in church? Because they have no organs.

474.   Why was the piano so good at making decisions? It had sharp keys!

475.   What do you get when you drop a piano on an army base? A flat major.

476.   What's a pig's favorite musical instrument? The saxophone.

477.   How do you make a band stand? Take away their chairs!

478.   What kind of music do mummies listen to? Wrap music.

479.   What did the music conductor say to the orchestra? "You're outstanding!"

480.   How do you make a tissue sing? Give it a high note!

Monster Jokes

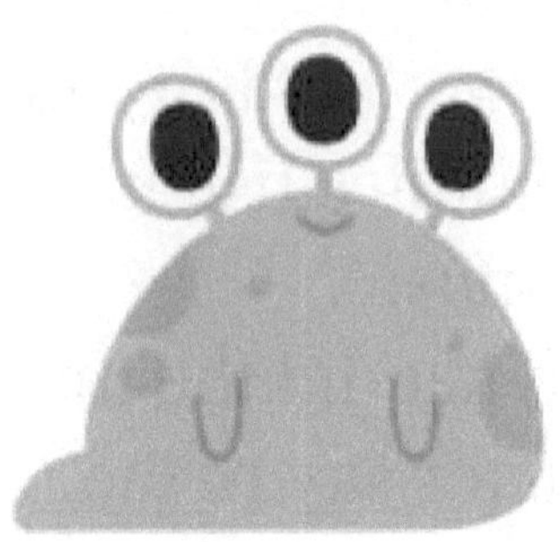

481.   What do you call a monster who tells jokes? A "funny-bone" monster!

482.   Why did the monster bring a ladder to school? Because he thought it was high school!

483.   What do you get when you cross a vampire with a snowman? Frostbite!

484.   Why don't monsters like fast food? Because they can't catch it!

485.   What do you call a polite and well-mannered monster? A "thank-ghoul."

486.   How do monsters pay for things? With "scream" credit cards!

487.   What do you call a monster who loves to dance? The "Boogieman"!

488.   What's a monster's favorite game? Hide and shriek!

489.   How does a monster like his coffee? With scream and sugar!

490.   Why did the monster bring a suitcase to the doctor? Because he

had a bad case of "the creeps"!

491.   What's a monster's favorite dessert? "I-scream" sundaes!

492.   How do you make a monster float? Add root beer, a scoop of ice scream, and a few screams!

493.   Why did the monster go to school with a ladder? Because he thought it was high school!

494.   What do you get when you cross a monster and a detective? A "scare"-chitect!

495.   Why don't monsters play hide and seek with ghosts? Because good

luck hiding when you're see-through!

496.   What's a monster's favorite subject in school? Scare-itmetry!

497.   Why did the monster bring a belt to the party? Because he wanted to "hold" it together!

498.   How do you calm down an angry monster? Give it a "coffin" break!

499.   What's a monster's favorite outdoor activity? "Scream" frisbee!

500.   Why did the monster bring a ladder to the library? Because he wanted to go to the "boo"-ks on the top shelf!

Parents Jokes

501. Why did the computer go to therapy with its parents? Because it had too many "motherboard" issues!

502. What do you call a dad who is also a vampire? A "dadpire"!

503. Why did the tomato turn red when it met the

parents? Because it saw the salad dressing!

504.   What do you get when you cross a dad and a cow? A "moo-ving" father!

505.   Why did the smartphone ground its kid? Because it lost its "cell-f control"!

506.   What did one wall say to the other wall at home? "I'll meet you at the corner!"

507.   Why don't parents tell secrets on a farm? Because the potatoes have "eyes," the corn has "ears," and the beans stalk!

508.   Why did the math book get in trouble with its parents? Because it

had too many
"problems"!

509.   What do you call a mom who can fix anything? A "supermum"!

510.   Why did the father clock get yelled at by his kids? Because he was always "watching" them!

511.   Why was the dad flower worried about its child? Because it was "petaled" to the metal!

512.   What did the baby corn say to its parent corn? "Where's my popcorn?"

513.   Why did the parent broom get an award? Because it was a "sweeping" success!

514.   Why did the computer keep turning off the Wi-Fi for the kids? Because it wanted some "byte" of quiet!

515.   What's a dad's favorite dessert? "Pop"corn!

516.   Why did the dad tomato give the kid tomato a hug? Because it was going through a "ketchup"!

517.   Why did the smartphone take its kid to school? Because it heard there was great "screen" time!

518.   What do you get when you cross a dad and a kangaroo? A "hop-timistic" parent!

519.   Why did the mom
broom bring the kid
broom to work? Because
it wanted to show it the
ropes!

520.   What's a parent's
favorite type of music?
"Rap" music, because it's
all about telling stories!

Time Jokes

521.　Why did the scarecrow become a great watchmaker? Because he was outstanding in his field of time!

522.　What's a clock's favorite game? Tick-tac-toe!

523.　How do you make a lemon laugh at a specific time? You tickle its citrus!

524.   Why did the computer keep looking at the clock? It couldn't resist the "byte" of time!

525.   What did one wall clock say to the other clock on the wall? "You hang around, and I'll go ahead and tick!"

526.   Why don't scientists trust atoms with timekeeping? Because they make up everything!

527.   How do you know when it's time to go to the dentist? When it's "tooth-hurty"!

528.   Why did the math book always look forward to lunchtime? Because it knew it had problems to solve!

529.   What's a snowman's
favorite part of the day?
The "chill" of the
morning!

530.   How did the
scientist ask for more
time? He put the
"request" in a bottle!

531.   What did the
calendar say to the clock?
"You have a lot of 'dates,'
don't you?"

532.   What did one
sundial say to the other?
"I can't help you with
that, I'm all about sunny
hours!"

533.   Why did the bicycle
fall over at noon?
Because it was two-tired!

534.   How does a
snowman get around

when it's not snowing?
By riding an "icicle"!
535.   Why was the broom
running out of time?
Because it was
"sweeping" too much!
536.   What did the digital
clock say to its mother?
"Look, no hands!"
537.   What's a bee's
favorite time of the day?
Buzz-ness hours!
538.   How do you make a
time machine out of a
car? You make it
"vroom" into the future!
539.   Why did the
calendar go to therapy? It
had too many "dates" and
couldn't keep up!
540.   How do you make
time fly? Throw a clock
out the window!

Country Jokes

541. Why did the scarecrow win an award in the country? Because he was outstanding in his field!

542. How does a farmer mend his overalls? With cabbage patches!

543. What do you call a cow with no legs? Ground beef!

544.   What kind of music do they play on the farm? Moosic!

545.   Why did the chicken join a band? Because it had the drumsticks!

546.   What do you get when you cross a snowman and a vampire in the country? Frostbite!

547.   Why did the tomato turn red? Because it saw the salad dressing!

548.   What's a scarecrow's favorite fruit? Strawberries!

549.   Why don't cows ever tell jokes? Because they're afraid of the "moo-dium"!

550.   What's a horse's favorite kind of story? A "neigh"-tale!

551.   How do you know if there's a chicken at your party? You'll find it with the "fowl" crowd!

552.   What do you call a country dog who can sing? A yodeling "dachshund"!

553.   Why did the farmer go to the bank? To get some "lawn" and order seeds!

554.   What's a sheep's favorite romantic movie? "Wooly in Love"!

555.   What do you call a pig that does karate? A "pork chop"!

556.   Why did the country road go to the doctor? Because it was a little "winding"!

557.   Why did the scarecrow become a successful politician in the country? Because he was outstanding at "corn"-municating!

558.   What did one haystack say to the other? "I'm not sure if we're baling hay or telling jokes!"

559.   Why don't farmers ever play hide and seek? Because good luck hiding when you're outstanding in your field!

560.   What's a country rabbit's favorite dance? The "hare"-do!

Birds Jokes

561.   Why did the bird go to school? To get a little "tweet"-ucation!

562.   What kind of bird is good at bowling? A "sparrow" (spare)!

563.   What do you get when you cross a bird and a snake? A "feathered" boa constrictor!

564.   What's a penguin's favorite relative? Aunt-Arctica!

565.   What do you call a bird who fixes things? A "mechanicraven"!

566.   How do crows stick together in a flock? Velcrow!

567.   What do you call a bird that's a magician? A "presto"-lark!

568.   Why did the seagull fly over the sea? Because if it flew over the bay, it would be a "bagel"!

569.   What kind of bird can fix your house? A "swan"-tractor!

570.   What do you call a bird that's sad? A blue-jay!

571.	Why don't birds use Facebook? Because they already have "tweet"er!

572.	What do you get when you cross a bird and a dog? A "parrot"-keet!

573.	What's a vulture's favorite snack? "Fast food" on the fly!

574.	Why do hummingbirds hum? Because they don't know the words!

575.	What kind of bird can write? A "pencil"-vania!

576.	How do birds stick together in a group? They use "glue-seum"!

577.	What do you call a bird in winter? A "brrrrd"!

578. What do you call a bird that lives at the North Pole? An "icicle"!

579. Why don't birds wear uniforms? Because they have "feather"-al rights!

580. What do you call a bird who can play the piano? A "keyboard" eagle!

Magic Jokes

581. Why did the magician take a ladder to the show? Because he wanted to see the "highlights"!

582. What's a magician's favorite type of music? Hocus Pocus!

583. What do you call a magician's rabbit when it escapes? A "hare"-raising adventure!

584.   Why did the magician go to school? To improve his "abracadabra"-spelling!

585.   What do you call a magician who lost his magic hat? "Brim"-ming with disappointment!

586.   Why was the magician so good at soccer? Because he had great "illu-soccer" skills!

587.   How does a magician ask for a favor? "Abraca-please"!

588.   Why did the magician take a suitcase to the show? Because he wanted to pack a "trick"!

589.   What do you call a magician's hot tub? A "bubbling cauldron"!

590.   Why did the magician always bring a pencil? In case he had to draw a "magic" circle!

591.   What do you call a magician's bunny that tells jokes? A "funny bunny"!

592.   Why did the magician bring a broom to the show? In case he needed to "sweep" the audience away!

593.   How do you make a tissue disappear? You "nose" the trick!

594.   Why did the magician bring a map to the show? In case he needed to find the "card"-inal directions!

595.   What do you call a magician who loves to

garden? A "thyme"-
traveling illusionist!

596.   How did the
magician become a
weather expert? He could
make "fog" disappear
instantly!

597.   Why did the
magician become a
gardener? He had a talent
for "plant"-ing secrets!

598.   What's a magician's
favorite game at the
park? Hide and "sleight
of hand"!

599.   Why don't
magicians ever play hide
and seek? Because they
always "vanish" before
they're found!

600.   What do you call a
magician's refrigerator?

A "chill"-dren's cabinet
of wonders!

Technology Jokes

601. Why did the computer go to therapy? It had too many "bytes" of emotional baggage!

602. What did the computer do at lunchtime? It had a byte to eat!

603. How do you organize a space party with computers? You "planet" in advance!

604.   Why was the math book sad when using a computer? Because it had too many problems!

605.   What did one smartphone say to the other? "You've got great 'cell'-f esteem!"

606.   Why don't scientists trust atoms? Because they make up everything, even computer jokes!

607.   How do you catch a computer mouse? Use some byte-sized cheese!

608.   Why do programmers always mix up Christmas and Halloween? Because Oct 31 == Dec 25!

609.   What's a computer's favorite snack? Micro-chips!

610.   Why was the computer cold? It left its Windows open!

611.   How do you comfort a JavaScript bug? You console it!

612.   What do you call a computer that sings? A Dell!

613.   What do you call a computer that can sing and dance? Adele!

614.   How does a computer get drunk? It takes screenshots!

615.   Why do computer scientists love nature? It has open-source code!

616.   What's a computer's favorite type of music? Heavy metal!

617.   How do robots send mail? Electronically!

618.   What's a robot's favorite snack? Computer chips!

619.   How do you fix a broken website? With a "bandwidth"-aid!

620.   What did the computer virus say to the other virus? "Do you want to go out and get a byte to eat?"

Toys Jokes

621.　What's a toy's favorite dessert? Jell-o!

622.　Why did the teddy bear say no to dessert? Because it was already stuffed!

623.　How do you organize a space-themed toy party? You "planet" in advance!

624.　What do you call a toy that loves to tell jokes? Silly Putty!

625.	Why don't toys ever get tired of playing hide and seek? Because they always have a "hidden" talent!

626.	What did one action figure say to the other? "You're my hero!"

627.	Why did the doll bring a ladder to the tea party? Because it wanted to meet "high tea" expectations!

628.	How does a toy fix a broken heart? With a "lovetool" kit!

629.	What do you call a toy that can do magic tricks? A wizard of "oohs" and "aahs"!

630.	Why did the toy robot go to school? To

get a "byte" of
knowledge!

631.   What's a toy's
favorite board game?
Connect Four-tunately!

632.   How do you make a
toy laugh? Tickle its
funny bone!

633.   Why did the toy
dinosaur refuse to share
its food? Because it was a
little "saur"!

634.   What did the toy
sailor say to the ocean?
"I've got my ship
together!"

635.   Why did the rubber
ducky bring an umbrella
to the bath? Because it
wanted to stay "quackers"
dry!

636.   What's a toy's
favorite kind of

sandwich? Peanut butter and "smile-y"!

637.   How do you make a toy roller coaster more exciting? You add a few "loop-de-loops"!

638.   Why did the toy truck stop in the middle of the road? Because it ran out of gas!

639.   What do you call a toy that can't stop telling stories? a "yarnspinner"!

640.   How do toys stay warm in the winter? They cuddle up with their "stuffy" friends!

Friend Ship Jokes

641. Why did the math book look sad? Because it had too many problems but found a friend to solve them!

642. What do you call two friends who love math? Algebros!

643. How do you make a tissue dance? You put a

little boogie in it, just like friends who dance together!

644.   Why did the scarecrow become such a great friend? Because he was outstanding in his field!

645.   What do you call a bear with no friends? A "bear"y lonely bear!

646.   Why did the two pencils become friends? Because they had a great "point" in common!

647.   What did one wall say to the other wall? "I'll meet you at the corner!" Friends always find a way to meet up!

648.   Why don't oysters donate to charity?

Because they're shellfish, unlike friends who share!

649.   How do you know when a friendship is sweet? When it's sugar and spice and everything nice!

650.   What's a panda's favorite way to make friends? By offering bamboo shoots and a "paws"corn of friendship!

651.   Why did the two pieces of bread become friends? Because they both had a lot of crust in each other!

652.   What did the one tree say to the other tree? "You're such a good friend; I'm rooting for you!"

653.   How did the two nuts become friends? They were both a little "nutty" about friendship!

654.   Why did the bicycle become friends with the motorcycle? Because they both had a "wheely" good time together!

655.   What do you call two birds in love? Tweet-hearts! True friends are like lovebirds.

656.   Why did the computer invite its friends to a party? Because it wanted to have a byte with them!

657.   How do you know when a friend is a good listener? When they're all ears!

658.   What do you call
friends who love science?
Lab partners in crime!

659.   Why did the tomato
turn red around its
friend? Because it saw
the salad dressing and
wanted to impress!

660.   What do you call
two friends who always
tell the best jokes?
Comedians in "laughter"
with each other!

Construction Jokes

661.   Why don't construction workers ever get lost? Because they always follow the "build"ing directions!

662.   How do construction workers party? They raise the roof!

663.   What do you call a hardworking group of construction vehicles? A "concrete" team!

664.   Why did the hammer go to school? To get a little "educe"-cation!

665.   How does a construction worker party? They "steel" the show!

666.   What's a construction worker's favorite type of music? Heavy metal!

667.   What do you call a grumpy piece of construction equipment? A "sour"ce of frustration!

668.   Why did the construction worker bring a ladder to the bar? Because they heard the drinks were on the house!

669.   How do construction workers stay cool in the

summer? They use
"asphalt" air
conditioning!

670. What did the
construction worker say
when they finished
building the puzzle?
"Nailed it!"

671. How do construction
workers stay in shape?
By lifting "concrete"
weights!

672. Why did the
construction worker get
in trouble with the
computer? They couldn't
find the "escape" key!

673. What's a
construction worker's
favorite dessert? A
"concrete" milkshake!

674. Why don't
construction workers ever

get tired of their jobs? Because they find them "riveting"!

675.	What do you call a friendly piece of construction equipment? A "bulldozer" of good deeds!

676.	Why was the construction worker always happy? Because they had great "beams" of positivity!

677.	How do construction workers stay organized? They use "blueprints" for their day!

678.	What do you call a dinosaur that's good at construction? A "try-ceratops"!

679.	Why was the construction worker so

good at math? Because
they had a strong
"foundation" in numbers!

680.   How do construction
workers make important
decisions? They
"concrete" and then go
with the flow!

Historical Figures

681.   Why did the mummy become a great comedian? Because he had a "wrapped" sense of humor!

682.   What did George Washington say to his troops before they crossed the Delaware

River? "Don't rock the boat!"

683.   Why did the ancient Greek philosopher go to the beach? To find some "shore" knowledge!

684.   How did Julius Caesar like his salad? "Et tu" crunchy!

685.   What did the caveman say to his friend during the Ice Age? "You crack me up!"

686.   Why was King Arthur's knights so good at math? Because they had "Excalibur" skills!

687.   Why was Joan of Arc always a hit at medieval parties? Because she had a "blazing" personality!

688.   How did Thomas Edison's light bulb feel when it finally worked? It was "lit" up with joy!

689.   What did Cleopatra say when she couldn't find her favorite chair? "I'm in de-Nile!"

690.   What did Galileo use to measure the stars? "Galilean" telescopes!

691.   How did Michelangelo get in shape for sculpting? He did a lot of "marble" workouts!

692.   Why was Sir Isaac Newton so good at soccer? He really knew how to use his "head"!

693.   How did Benjamin Franklin feel when he

discovered electricity?
He was shocked!

694.   What's Sherlock
Holmes' favorite game at
the beach?
"Sand"scapades!

695.   What did Amelia
Earhart say when she
finished her
groundbreaking flight?
"I'm plane tired!"

696.   What did the ancient
Egyptian pharaoh say
when he needed a break
from ruling? "I need a
"pyra-mid" time off!"

697.   Why did Leonardo
da Vinci make a great
chef? Because he could
"draw" up fantastic
recipes!

698.   How did
Christopher Columbus

navigate the ocean? He used "sea"-crets!

699.   What did Marco Polo say after his journey to the Far East? "I need a long "Polo" break!"

700.   Why did Albert Einstein bring a ladder to the library? Because he wanted to learn about "relativity"!

Gnomes Jokes

701.   What do you call a gnome who tells jokes? A "pun"-tomime gnome!

702.   Why did the gnome bring a ladder to the garden? Because he wanted to go to the "next level"!

703.   How do gnomes
stay cool in the
summertime? They use
their "shady"
personalities!

704.   What's a gnome's
favorite type of music?
"Rock" and roll!

705.   What do you get
when you cross a gnome
with a leprechaun? A
"little" bit of magic!

706.   Why did the gnome
bring a map to the forest?
He didn't want to get
"gnome"-adic!

707.   What did the gnome
say to the tree in the
forest? "You're really
branching out!"

708.   How do gnomes
stay in shape? They do
"mushroom" workouts!

709.   What do you call a gnome who's great with technology? A "gnome"-puter whiz!

710.   What did one gnome say to the other when they found a treasure chest? "We struck 'gnome' gold!"

711.   How do gnomes send letters to each other? By "mushroom" delivery!

712.   What do you call a gnome who loves to dance? A "twinkle-toes gnome"!

713.   Why did the gnome bring a rake to the party? Because he wanted to "leaf" a good impression!

714.   What's a gnome's favorite game? Hide and "gno-seek"!

715.   How do gnomes make wishes? They toss a coin in the "well" and hope for the best!

716.   What's a gnome's favorite movie genre? "Gnome"-coms (gnome comedies)!

717.   Why did the gnome become a gardener? Because he had a green thumb!

718.   What do you call a gnome who's always happy? "Gno-more" the Glee Gnome!

719.   How did the gnome win the race in the garden? He took a "short" cut!

720.   Why do gnomes always make great friends? Because they're

"gnome"-orous and kind-
hearted!

Pets vs. Wildlife

721.   Why did the pet cat join the wildlife documentary team? Because it wanted to be a "purr"-ofessional observer!

722.   What's a cat's favorite wildlife TV show? "Meow-ture Planet"!

723.   Why did the squirrel invite the pet hamster to the forest? Because they both wanted to "rodent" their time wisely!

724.   How does a pet dog feel about watching birds in the garden? He thinks

it's "pawsitively"
fascinating!

725.   What do you call a
pet parrot's attempt to
mimic a wild bird's call?
A "tweet"-mismatch!

726.   Why did the pet
rabbit bring a backpack
to the wildlife preserve?
Because it wanted to
have a "hare"-raising
adventure!

727.   How do pet fish feel
about wildlife in the
ocean? They think it's
"fintastic"!

728.   What do you call a
pet snake's reaction to
seeing a wild snake on
TV? A "hiss-terical"
moment!

729.   Why did the pet
guinea pig start a wildlife

blog? Because it wanted to share its "wheek"-end wildlife adventures!

730.   What did the pet lizard say when it met a wild chameleon? "You're really good at blending in!"

731.   How does a pet turtle feel when it watches a video about tortoises in the wild? It's "shell-shocked" by the similarities!

732.   What do you call a pet ferret's dream of joining a group of wild ferrets? A "ferret-tale" adventure!

733.   Why do pet birds enjoy watching wild birds outside the window? Because it's like

their "feathered" friends
on TV!

734.   What's a pet
goldfish's opinion of the
fish in the wild? "They're
the originals, but I've got
a cool tank!"

735.   Why did the pet
hamster invite a wild
gerbil to its birthday
party? Because it wanted
to "rodent" the
celebration!

736.   How do pet hermit
crabs feel when they see
wild hermit crabs on the
beach? They're "shell-
shocked" by the
similarities!

737.   What's a pet turtle's
favorite wildlife show?
"Turtley Awesome
Adventures"!

738.   Why did the pet snake watch a documentary about wild pythons? To learn more about its "long-distance" relatives!

739.   How did the pet rabbit react when it saw wild bunnies in the garden? It thought it was hosting a "bunny" convention!

740.   What do you call a pet cat's reaction to seeing a wild big cat on TV? A "purr"-spective on their family history!

Unusual Hobbies

741.   Why did the kid become a professional cloud watcher? Because they wanted to reach new "heights" in their hobbies!

742.   What's a pirate's favorite unusual hobby? "Arrr"-chery!

743.   Why did the soccer player take up extreme ironing? Because they wanted to kick wrinkles to the curb!

744.   What did the artist say about their unusual hobby of painting with spaghetti noodles? "It's a

real pasta-cinating experience!"

745.   Why did the scientist take up underwater basket weaving? Because they wanted to dive into a new field of study!

746.   What do you call someone who collects rubber ducks as a hobby? A "quack-tastic" enthusiast!

747.   Why did the gardener start a club for extreme topiary sculpting? Because they wanted to hedge their bets on fun!

748.   How did the kid get into the hobby of collecting vintage alarm clocks? They wanted to

"tick" all the boxes of time!

749.   What did the detective say about their hobby of solving jigsaw puzzles in the dark? "It's a real mystery in the making!"

750.   Why did the astronaut pick up the hobby of knitting in zero gravity? Because they needed an out-of-this-world scarf!

751.   What do you call someone who collects rare and exotic doorknobs as a hobby? A "turn-tastic" collector!

752.   Why did the chef take up the hobby of extreme pancake

flipping? Because they wanted to flip for joy!

753.   What did the beekeeper say about their unusual hobby of honeycomb art? "It's the bee's knees of creativity!"

754.   Why did the surfer decide to pursue sandcastle architecture as a hobby? Because they wanted to ride the wave of design!

755.   What do you call someone who practices competitive hula hooping? A "spin-sational" athlete!

756.   Why did the archaeologist start a club for fossilized bug collecting? Because they

wanted to explore the ancient insect world!

757.   How did the daredevil get into the hobby of tightrope walking over hot lava? They liked to live life on the edge!

758.   What did the musician say about their unusual hobby of composing songs for rubber chickens? "It's eggstremely entertaining!"

759.   Why did the spelunker take up the hobby of rock whispering? Because they wanted to keep their ear to the ground!

760.   What do you call someone who collects

antique toasters as a
hobby? A "toast"-orian!

Circus Jokes

761. Why did the clown bring a ladder to the circus? Because he wanted to go to great heights in comedy!

762. What do you call a bear that loves to tell jokes at the circus? A "stand-up" comedian!

763. How do circus lions send messages to each other? By "snail mail"!

764. Why did the trapeze artist bring a parachute to the circus? Just in case they wanted to "drop" in unexpectedly!

765. What do you call a circus elephant that's

good at math? An "add-a-
phant"!

766.   How do circus
acrobats stay cool during
their performances? They
use "cool flips"!

767.   What's a tightrope
walker's favorite type of
music? Anything with a
"balancing" beat!

768.   Why did the circus
clown bring a suitcase to
the show? Because he
heard the laughter was so
good, he wanted to
"pack" some to take
home!

769.   What's a lion tamer's
favorite kind of
sandwich? Peanut butter
and "roar-jelly"!

770.   How do circus
elephants talk to each

other long-distance? With "ele-phone" calls!

771.   Why did the magician bring a broom to the circus? Because he wanted to "sweep" the audience off their feet!

772.   What did the circus ringmaster say when he couldn't find his top hat? "I'm having a 'hat-tastrophe'!"

773.   Why did the circus clown ride a unicycle? Because he couldn't afford a "bi-cycle"!

774.   How do circus horses stay in shape? With plenty of "stable" exercises!

775.   What's a contortionist's favorite

snack at the circus?
"Pretzel"-coated popcorn!
776.   Why did the circus
seal bring a backpack to
the performance?
Because he wanted to
"seal" his lunch!
777.   How do circus
strongmen make coffee?
They use "muscle-brew"!
778.   Why did the circus
penguin get a part-time
job as a snow cone
vendor? To keep cool in
the heat of the show!
779.   What did the circus
magician say when he
made his assistant
disappear? "She's just
'vanish-tastic'!"
780.   How do circus
clowns stay entertained

in their downtime? They
"juggle" with ideas!

Amusement Park Jokes

781.   Why did the roller coaster bring a pencil to the amusement park? To draw its own path of excitement!

782.   What's a pirate's favorite ride at the amusement park? The "yarrrrrrrrr"-go-round!

783.   What did the cotton candy say to the amusement park ride? "You make me feel so spun!"

784.   Why did the amusement park employee bring a ladder to work? Because they

wanted to climb the corporate ladder!

785.   How did the amusement park clown become the star of the show? He had great "circus-tances"!

786.   What's a skeleton's favorite ride at the amusement park? The roller "ghoster"!

787.   Why did the amusement park carousel attend school? To get a little "horse" sense!

788.   What's a vampire's favorite ride at the amusement park? The "fang"-tastic Ferris wheel!

789.   Why did the amusement park snack bar run out of ice cream?

Because they couldn't
"scoop" fast enough!

790.   What's a tiger's favorite ride at the amusement park? The "roar"-ler coaster!

791.   How do amusement park rides communicate with each other? They use "scream" time technology!

792.   Why did the amusement park magician make all the cotton candy disappear? Because he wanted to create a "sweet" illusion!

793.   What do you call a roller coaster enthusiast? A "loop"-er!

794.   Why did the amusement park roller coaster bring a jacket to

the ride? Because it's
always a little "chilly" up
there!

795.   How do you make a
cotton candy dance at the
amusement park? Give it
a little "spin"!

796.   What's a bear's
favorite ride at the
amusement park? The
"bear"-is wheel!

797.   Why did the
amusement park's hot
dog vendor become
famous? Because they
had a "dog"-gone good
recipe!

798.   What's an octopus's
favorite ride at the
amusement park? The
"tentacle"-twisting ride!

799.   Why did the
amusement park water

ride get an award?
Because it made a real
"splash" at the ceremony!
800.   How do you keep an
amusement park ticket
safe? You "ride"-e it out
in your pocket!

www.ingramcontent.com/pod-product-compliance
Lightning Source LLC
Chambersburg PA
CBHW061448150726
47987CB00001B/379